Ladybird I'm **Ready...** for **Phonics!**

Note to parents, carers and teachers

Ladybird I'm Ready for Phonics is a series of phonic reading books that have been carefully written to give gradual, structured practice of the synthetic phonics programme your child is learning at school.

Each book focuses on a set of phonemes (sounds) together with their graphemes (letters). The books also provide practice of common tricky words, such as **the** and **said**, that cannot be sounded out.

The series closely follows the order that your child is taught phonics in school, from initial letter sounds to key phonemes and beyond. It helps to build reading confidence through practice of these phonics building blocks, and reinforces school learning in a fun way.

Ideas for use

- Children learn best when reading is a fun experience. Read the book together and give your child plenty of praise and encouragement.

- Help your child identify and sound out the phonemes (sounds) in any words he is having difficulty reading. Then, blend these sounds together to read the word.

- Talk about the story words and tricky words at the end of each story to reinforce learning.

For more information and advice on synthetic phonics and school book banding, visit **www.ladybird.com/phonics**

Book Band 2

Level 6 builds on the sounds learnt in levels 1 to 5
and introduces new sounds and their letter representations:

ch sh th th ng

(soft) (hard)

Special features:

repetition of sounds
in different words

short sentences with
simple language

Meg was in a big den with a lot of egg shells.

This is a big chick, Dash.

That is not a chick, Meg.

Thud!
Bash!

8

9

Story Words

Can you match these words to the pictures below?

Bash   bush

Dash   long thing

muck

Tricky Words

These tricky words are in the story you have just read. They cannot be phonetically sounded out. Can you memorize them and read them super fast?

into   I

the   to

was

31

summary page to
reinforce learning

Written by Catherine Baker
Illustrated by Ian Cunliffe

Phonics and Book Banding Consultant: Kate Ruttle

A catalogue record for this book is available from the British Library

Published by Ladybird Books Ltd
80 Strand, London, WC2R 0RL
A Penguin Company

001

ISBN: 978-0-72327-542-8
Printed in China

Ladybird I'm Ready... for Phonics!

Dash and the Thing

Meg was not in the den.

Dash, go and get Meg.

7

Meg was in a big den with a lot of egg shells.

This is a big chick, Dash.

Thud!
Bash!

Then they got a shock.

Run, Meg!
Go back to Mum.

Meg shot off.
Dash ran in a ring.

If I run
in rings, I
will get ill.

Bang! The big thing fell
with a thud.

Meg and Dash got back
to the den.

That was such
a shock.

Mum had a hug with them.

Dash is fab!

Story Words

Can you match these words to the pictures below?

Dash

Meg

Mum

den

egg shells

fangs

Tricky Words

These tricky words are in the story you have just read. They cannot be phonetically sounded out. Can you memorize them and read them super fast?

go

to

they

the

I

be

was

Ladybird I'm Ready...
for Phonics!

Big Bad Bash

Bash is the king of big and bad.

But then Dash got
a long, thin thing.

Bash hung on to
the long thing.

Bash had to tug and tug.

Bash fell into the muck
with a thud!

Story Words

Can you match these words to the pictures below?

Bash	bush
Dash	long thing
muck	

Tricky Words

These tricky words are in the story you have just read. They cannot be phonetically sounded out. Can you memorize them and read them super fast?

into

I

the

to

was

Collect all
Ladybird I'm Ready...
for Phonics!

Captain Comet's Space Party

9780723275374

Nut Naps!

9780723275381

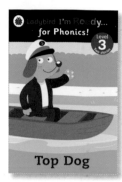

Top Dog

9780723275398

Huff! Puff! Run!

9780723275404

Fix It Vets

9780723275411

Dash is Fab!

9780723275428

Say the Sounds

9780723271598

Flashcards

9780723272069

Available on the **App Store**

Ladybird I'm Ready for...
apps are now available for
iPad, iPhone and iPod touch.

Apps also available on Android devices